Marianne's Magical Journey

by
Kathleen Rand
&
Chandavictoria Cleveland

RESOURCE *Publications* • Eugene, Oregon

Resource Publications
A division of Wipf and Stock Publishers
199 W 8th Ave, Suite 3
Eugene, OR 97401

Marianne's Magical Journey
By Cleveland, Chandavictoria and Rand, Kathleen
Copyright©1995 by Cleveland, Chandavictoria
ISBN 13: 978-1-5326-7691-8
Publication date 12/4/2018
Previously published by Monterey Pacific Publishing, 1995

This book is dedicated to all children of the world
who hold magic in their hearts...

A long time ago in a faraway land, or was it really around the corner? Oh well, no matter. This is a story about a little girl named Marianne. She's about your age really, maybe a year or two older, but she's not much older at all.

Marianne lived in a normal house, went to a normal school, had a normal family and had a normal life; except for one thing. She was sad! Marianne really didn't know why she was sad. She just knew that she was sad. Can you imagine that? Marianne was sad because she was mixed up about things. She went to school and she couldn't figure out why she had to go to school. She did things with her family, but she wasn't quite sure why they did the kinds of things they did. The more Marianne thought about why things were like they were, the more mixed up and sad she became.

One day, on her way home from school, Marianne passed by a pet store. She had taken a detour that day; it was only a little out of the way. As Marianne walked past the pet store, she noticed a brightly-colored bird. Now this was no ordinary bird. It was bright green with red on its back and a yellow head. What was so unusual about the bird was that he smiled and waved at Marianne as she walked past him. Marianne stopped dead in her tracks.

"Could a bird wave at me?" Marianne asked herself. Marianne returned to the window of the pet store. The brightly-colored bird smiled again, and motioned with his wing for her to come into the store.

"I wonder if I should go in?" Marianne asked herself. "Why not?" And with a skip in her step, Marianne went inside the store. Inside there were many animals. The man behind the counter said, "Welcome, please come in and browse." So Marianne went over to the bird's cage. She peered down into the cage and to her surprise the bird spoke to her! He spoke no louder than a whisper,

"I can feel that you are sad. Please tell me why you are sad.

1

I like you. I don't speak to just anyone."

"What is your name?" asked Marianne.

"My name is Banu" replied the bird.

"You really are beautiful to look at." offered Marianne.

"Let me tell you a story" said Banu. Marianne sat down on a bag of bird seed and began to listen to Banu's story.

"I come from the jungle, near a big river called the Amazon. I love the jungle. We were all so happy there. Imagine having all your friends live so close to you that all you have to do is call their name and they are there. I loved my home in the Amazon, but a while ago, I was flying with my bird friends and I was captured by some men. They put me in a dark box and it was hard for me to breathe. Next, I was put into a very small cage and then I came to this place. I think this is some kind of place that sells animals. I watch all the people and animals that come and go in front of this window. I saw you walk by my window. You looked so sad that I had to do something. You see, in the jungle no one is allowed to be sad. Matori sees to that! This is why I can be happy even though I am stuck in a cage. I want you to tell me why you are so sad. I think maybe that I can help you. Will you help Banu?" asked the bird with a questioning look on his face.

"Wow, what a story! Who is Matori? Where is the Amazon? What kind of animals live there?" asked Marianne. She continued, "I will tell you why I am so sad." She shifted her weight on the sack of bird seed and glanced around the pet store to see if anyone might be listening. You see, Marianne could be very shy at times. And she didn't want just anyone to hear her story.

"You know, Banu, I guess I'm so sad because I can't figure out why I have to do the things I do all day. Why do people have to do things at certain times of the day? I wonder too much about things, at least that's what my mom says. I am glad you asked me why I am so sad. I needed to tell someone," Marianne said. "How come no one is allowed to be sad in the jungle and who is Matori anyway? Is he the jungle police or something?" asked Marianne.

2

Banu giggled slightly as he fluffed his feathers and scooted over to the edge of his cage. "Will you scratch my neck?" asked Banu. He stretched his neck and Marianne found herself scratching it.

"Matori is the wise man of the jungle. He helps us all to understand what a wonderful thing life is. He taught us the meaning of life in the jungle. And once we learned what that secret was, no one could be sad," explained Banu.

Marianne glanced at the watch she wore on her wrist and counted the hours and minutes just the way her mom had taught her. Reading a watch was hard for her as she was just learning to tell time.

"Oh my goodness, it is time for me to go, Banu. If I'm late my mom will worry about me," explained Marianne. "Can I come and see you tomorrow and will you tell me more about your home?" asked Marianne.

"Yes, of course," said Banu as he bowed to her and stretched out his wings. "I look forward to seeing you tomorrow." Saying good-bye, Marianne left the store with a smile on her face. "Maybe I can help her after all," Banu thought to himself.

The next day after school, Marianne found herself taking her shortcut home and went to the pet store. Once again, Banu was in his cage. He smiled at her as she approached his window and waved to him. "How are you today, Banu? I have been thinking about you ever since I was here yesterday. I want to hear more about your home in the Amazon."

Banu stretched his wings again in his now familiar way and he asked Marianne to sit down and he would tell her more about his home. "There is something you must understand about the rain forest," said Banu. "It is a special place because it is filled with magic. All the creatures who live there believe that anything is possible if they believe in it strongly enough. This is how I can still be happy away from my home, because I know that one day I will return there and be with Matori and all my friends," explained Banu.

"I wish I could be happy like you," said Marianne. "It would be nice to have a real place that believed in magic. I believe in magic, but my mom says that there's no such thing. How wonderful your life must have been there," said Marianne. "If only I could go with you to such a place one day."

"If I could get to Matori, he could show you his magic," explained Banu. Banu stopped talking and got a strange look on his face. He seemed to be concentrating on something. Marianne could not quite figure out what it was. She shifted uncomfortably on the sack she was sitting on.

"I hope I didn't ask him too many questions," Marianne said to herself. She was always being told to be quiet and not ask so many questions. Banu stretched his wings and smiled.

"How would you like to go with me to the Amazon, become a bird like me and learn how to be happy?" asked Banu.

"I would love to!" exclaimed Marianne as she jumped up and down. "I would love to!"

"If only I could get to Matori," pondered Banu. "If only..."

"I'll go!" whispered a tiny voice below Banu. "I've been listening and I would be honored to go." Marianne and Banu were looking all around for the location of the tiny voice. Finally Banu smiled and picked up a tiny flea from his feathers. The flea waved his legs about and jumped up and down, "I would be honored to find Matori for you!"

Now it just so happens that the flea flew and flew and hopped and flew but he got very tired. He knew that he must continue on his journey to find Matori. He knew which way was south and he kept heading in that direction. Soon, however, he was so tired that he could not go any further. The flea managed to get the attention of a butterfly that just happened to be flying overhead. The flea told his tale to the butterfly who had heard legends of the wise man Matori. And do you know what?

4

The butterfly told the flea that she would find Matori for him. The flea died while looking up into the face of that butterfly for he knew that he had done his best. The butterfly wiped away her tears, stretched and fluttered her wings toward the sun. She got her bearings and headed south.

The butterfly flew for many days. She was buffeted by wind and rain and still she flew. Eventually she became trapped in a spider's web. The butterfly pleaded with the spider to let her go, but the spider was very hungry; and although he felt sorry for the butterfly he did not let her go since this is nature's way. However, a nice bright firefly was passing by and heard the pleas of the butterfly. "Don't worry, butterfly, I will find Matori!" she called and she flew off to the south. The firefly was very resourceful and she had the wind help her fly very far and fast to the south. She knew that she was close to the Amazon because the air was thicker and hotter and there were many trees. On and on she flew, but the firefly got so tired she fell, hit her head and was lying on the ground unconscious!

The firefly lay there for a long time. Then she felt a gentle breeze along her body. She opened her eyes. She looked up into the face of a bird; a sparrow to be exact. It was a kind face. So she told her story to the bird. She told the bird that she must find Matori. The bird smiled and suddenly a wind ruffled the bird's feathers. The firefly blinked because the bird's face had changed. It was now the face of a man.

The man smiled, picked up the firefly and whispered to her, "Rest now, my friend. You have succeeded. I am Matori. I will help Banu and his new friend." The surrounding leaves rustled and the firefly was alone. Matori was gone.

Banu sat in his cage, telling Marianne about his mother and how wonderful she was, when he paused in his story. Banu strained his head as if listening very hard for something. Suddenly, Marianne saw Banu's smile get bigger than she had ever seen (she still wasn't quite sure how birds could smile anyway). Banu turned, looked at Marianne and simply said, "Matori has come." But Marianne could not see anyone. To her,

5

the pet store still looked the same.

"Where is he, Banu?" asked Marianne.

"He has come. Take me out of my cage. It is alright, the man won't see," said Banu. So Marianne reached into Banu's cage and Banu stepped onto her finger. Suddenly Marianne felt a breeze in the store. She wondered how a breeze could be in a building, and there, next to her, was a man; a man with leaves on his head, a man with a very warm smile.

He extended his hand towards Marianne and Banu and said, "Come with me. I am Matori. I have heard your story from a firefly and I have come to help. Come to the jungle with me and learn what it means to be happy." Marianne was so surprised at what happened next. She took Matori's hand and the room seemed to spin. The next thing she knew, she was in a forest.

"How did I get here?" asked Marianne.

"Do you believe in magic?" asked Matori.

"Yes, I do," said Marianne.

"Then that is how you came to be here," explained Matori.

Banu immediately jumped from Marianne's hand and flew up to the nearest tree branch. It had been so long since he had been able to fly.

"Thank you, Matori! Look, Marianne, this is the rain forest. This is the Amazon. This is my home," cried Banu. "Matori, please watch out for her. I will be back. I have to see my mother!" And Banu was off in a flash. Marianne was a little scared in the forest with a stranger.

"Don't be afraid," Matori said calmly. "Now close your eyes. I have a surprise for you!" Marianne felt the breeze again. "Now open your eyes," said Matori. Marianne opened her eyes, but she could not believe what she saw! She had wings. She was a bird just like Banu.

"Wow!" exclaimed Marianne. This was the best thing that ever happened to her.

Marianne stretched her wings. She was amazed at how light her body felt. "Is this what it feels like to be a bird? It must," she thought to herself, "I am a bird!"

Matori let Marianne perch on his shoulder as he showed her his jungle home. Marianne felt that the rain forest was trees on top of trees and then more trees. She noticed that there was life everywhere. There were bugs on the ground. There were brightly colored flowers everywhere and there were many different kinds of plants, birds, monkeys and, oh...everything was so alive. Soon Banu returned with a whole flock of birds. Marianne had never seen him so happy. Banu introduced Marianne to his entire family, especially his mother. The next thing Marianne knew, Matori's magic wind had come back and Matori was once again a bird, this time a parrot. With Matori's and Banu's help, Marianne learned to fly.

"What an experience!" she shouted as she flew with Banu's family. "I had no idea I could ever feel so free," explained Marianne.

Matori had a knowing smile on his face as he and Banu showed Marianne their magical home. Marianne believed that the rain forest was truly a magical place, a place of wonder, a place that was alive. Soon after, Marianne began feeling as if she had always been a bird and for many days she soared the skies, played and learned about the rain forest and animals from Matori and Banu. But as time went on, she began to wonder about her own family back home in the city. Was her mother missing her, just as Banu has missed his mother? She had never been so happy in her life! She had forgotten all about being sad. She wondered what had happened to her that made her forget about being sad all of the time. Marianne decided that she would ask Matori.

"How come since I came to the rain forest, I have forgotten all about being sad? I love it here, but I miss my mom. I don't want to be sad like I was before."

Matori settled down on the branch of a tree, for he was still a parrot. "Let me tell you the secret of life, Marianne. By learning this, wherever you go you will always be happy because it is the true magic of the world. Look around you. Everything is alive. How do you feel when you look at the life around you?" asked Matori.

"I feel like I am part of all this stuff that is going on here. I don't feel left out, I feel happy," said Marianne.

"That feeling of being a part of everything is the secret of life. What I mean, Marianne, is that by coming to the rain forest you have learned to become a part of life, not outside of it," explained Matori. "Do you understand?"

"Kind of," said Marianne. "But how can I be a part of all this? I am really a girl, not a bird."

"It does not matter if you are a girl, a bird or a bug. We are all part of this pattern of life," Matori explained, "just like the flea & the butterfly who gave their lives to bring me to Banu and to you. You are both a part of this pattern, too. So if you remember that everyone, no matter how big or small, is woven together into the pattern of life, you are never alone and can never be sad!"

"I get it!" said Marianne. "If I understand that I am a part of this whole thing of being alive, I'm not alone. I remember that when I was feeling alone, I got sad. Matori, what a wonderful secret you have shared with me! Why don't people remember this more often?" asked Marianne.

"Because people have left their forest homes," said Matori. "I feel sad for all the living creatures who feel alone when they really are not. Marianne, are you ready to stay here and be a bird with us?"

"I would really like to," said Marianne, "but I miss my mom. I love being a bird, but I miss my family, just like Banu did!"

"Then go and say your good-byes to Banu and his family, Marianne, and return to me by sunset." And then Matori was gone.

Marianne spent the entire day with Banu and his family.

She saw the wonder of the rain forest and she vowed to herself that when she returned home, she would remember that she was part of the pattern of life and she would help protect the rain forest and preserve the secret of life. At sunset she found Matori waiting for her. Matori smiled at her and told her to remember what she had learned, to remember the magic of life. A gentle breeze ruffled Marianne's feathers. The forest began to spin and the next thing Marianne saw was her reflection in the pet store window. She was a girl again.

"Yippee," hollered Marianne, and she ran fast toward home.

From that time on, no one could ever remember Marianne being sad. She was always happy, always helping others. Strangely, no one had even known she had been gone. "Matori's magic must have made people forget I was gone," thought Marianne.

Every once in a while Marianne would again disappear for a time, but no one would notice because they were too busy watching a flock of brightly colored birds flying about the city. People wondered where the birds came from and where they went—but not Marianne, because she knew the secret!

The End

Kathleen Rand would like to thank the following people...

Chandavictoria for your great imagination.
Helen Reed for your artistic intuition.
Lujean Quilici for listening to me babble.
Fiana Anderson for putting up with me
and
Yubby, Puddy, and Precious for your patience.
and
Toni Buhrke Haggard, of course!

About the Authors

Kathleen Rand and her daughter Chandavictoria Cleveland have joined forces in this their first children's book. Kathleen and Chandavictoria make their home in Reno, Nevada. When they are not writing stories they both enjoy tennis, travel and meeting people. This is the first book in a series of many adventures of Matori, Marianne and Banu!!